Dragon Slayers' Academy™ 3

CLASS TRIP to the CAVE of DOOM

By Kate McMullan
Illustrated by Bill Basso

SCHOLASTIC INC.

New York Toronto London Auckland Sydney
Mexico City New Delhi Hong Kong Buenos Aires

For Jeff Hall
—K. McM.

For my dearest Marie
—B.B

ISBN 0-439-14908-8

23 22 21 20 19 18 17 16 15 14   8 9/0

Printed in the U.S.A.   40

First Scholastic printing, February 2004

Chapter 1

link! Clink! Clink! Mordred, the headmaster of Dragon Slayers' Academy, banged his spoon on his glass. *Clink! Clink! Clink!*

"Boys!" Mordred's loud voice filled the DSA dining hall. "I have a surprise for you!"

Egad! thought Wiglaf. *What now?* Mordred's last surprise had been a scrubbing party. Wiglaf had been up half the night, working on the stew pot.

"Maybe Uncle Mordred caught the boys who threw his boots into the moat," Angus whispered to Wiglaf. Angus was the headmaster's nephew. But Wiglaf didn't hold that against him. "Or maybe," Angus went on, "he found out who dropped Sir Mort's false teeth into the cider jug."

"Shh, Angus!" said Erica, who was also Wiglaf's friend. "We're supposed to be—"

"QUIIIIIET!" Mordred roared.

A hush fell over the dining hall.

"That's better." The headmaster smiled. His gold tooth shone in the torchlight. "Now, as you know, Wiglaf has killed two dragons."

Wiglaf gasped. Could it be? Was Mordred at last going to honor him as a hero?

"But tell me, boys," Mordred continued. "Did Wiglaf bring back any dragon gold for *me*?"

"Nooooooo!" the DSA students cried.

Wiglaf slid down in his seat. He should have known! Mordred was only picking on him—again.

Wiglaf was sick of being picked on. Back home, his twelve brothers picked on him all the time. They called him Runt, because he was small for his age. They made fun of his carrot-colored hair and his pet pig, Daisy. They teased him about his tender-hearted ways.

Wiglaf had hoped that things would be better at school. He had come to DSA to learn to be a hero. And he *had* killed two dragons. A young one named Gorzil and his mother, Seetha. But the truth was, Wiglaf had killed them by accident. He could never have cut off their heads. Or poked his sword into their guts. The very thought of blood made Wiglaf sick to his stomach. Still, he *had* killed them. That should count for something. And he was the only boy at DSA ever to kill *any* dragon. But Mordred didn't care about dead dragons. All he cared about was getting his hands on their gold.

"Wiglaf brought me no gold," Mordred moaned softly. "No gold." Then his violet eyes lit up. "But rumors are flying!" he exclaimed. "Villagers in Ratswhiskers say that before Seetha died, she hid all her gold in a cave in the Dark Forest."

Erica jumped up. "Let *me* go to that cave, sir!" she cried. "I shall bring you Seetha's gold!"

Wiglaf smiled. Erica was so gung ho about dragon slaying. Mordred did not let girls into his school. So Erica cut her straight brown hair and dressed as a boy so she could go to DSA. Everyone there called her Eric. Only Wiglaf knew that she was really Erica. Princess Erica, as a matter of fact.

"You *shall* go, Eric," Mordred roared. "*All* of you are going on a class trip to the Dark Forest! That is my surprise! All of you are going to hunt for Seetha's gold!"

"Hooray!" Erica cried.

A few others cheered. But not Wiglaf. The

Dark Forest was not exactly a vacation spot. It was *dark*, for one thing. And very scary.

"You shall meet in the castle yard tomorrow morning," Mordred continued. "Then you shall march into the Dark Forest. And the boy who finds Seetha's gold..." Mordred rubbed his hands together. "...will get a great big *prize!*"

"Hooray!" everyone cheered this time.

"Wiggie!" Erica called over the cheering. "I am sure to find Seetha's gold, so you and Angus stick with me. That way, you can share the prize!"

Wiglaf nodded. If only the prize were some of Seetha's gold. Then he could pay the seven pennies he still owed DSA for his tuition. He could send some money to his greedy family back in Pinwick. And maybe—just maybe—if he found Seetha's gold, Mordred would stop picking on him.

Chapter 2

ump, boys! Higher!" Coach Plungett, the DSA slaying teacher, called early the next morning. His brown pageboy wig blew in the breeze as he counted jumping jacks. "Ninety-one! Ninety-two! Exercise will make you manly men, like me!"

Wiglaf had never done so many jumping jacks. His arms were ready to drop off.

But Coach kept counting. "One hundred three!" he cried. "Jumping is a manly way to warm up on a chilly morning!"

The boys had stumbled into the castle yard

before sunup. Coach Plungett put them into groups. Coach was the leader of the Bloodhounds. Wiglaf was a Bloodhound. Angus and Erica were Bloodhounds, too. So were the big Marley brothers: Barley, Charlie, Farley, and Harley.

Wiglaf looked over at the Marleys doing sloppy jumping jacks. He couldn't tell one brother from another. They never said much. They were known for playing jokes. Wiglaf was pretty sure the Marleys had thrown Mordred's boots into the moat.

"One hundred twenty!" Coach counted.

"I cannot...do any...more!" Wiglaf gasped.

"This is nothing," yelled Erica. She was jumping next to him. "I once did six hundred jumping jacks. And I wasn't even out of breath."

Wiglaf could barely hear what Erica was saying. Her tool belt was clanking too loudly.

She had sent away for it from the Sir Lancelot Fan Club catalog. All sorts of fine dragon-slaying equipment hung from the wide silver belt. A canteen. A collapsible goblet. A spyglass. A magnifying glass. A rope. A small copy of *The Sir Lancelot Handbook*. A mini-torch. A pack of dry sticks for starting fires. A spare sword. A lice comb. And a toothpick.

All Wiglaf had was a beat-up sword. His lucky rag was tied to the handle. But now, as he did his one hundred eighty-second jumping jack, he was just as glad not to be wearing a heavy tool belt.

"Where is Mordred anyway?" Erica asked.

"You know Uncle Mordred hates to get up before noon," Angus answered.

Angus moved his arms up and down as Coach counted. But he kept his feet planted on the ground. Since Angus was Mordred's nephew, Coach Plungett pretended not to notice.

"Two hundred!" Coach called. "Halt!"

Wiglaf stopped jumping. He thought *halt* was the most beautiful word he'd ever heard.

"Now hit the ground for two hundred push-ups!" Coach called.

Wiglaf groaned. Was Coach trying to slay them?

Luckily, at that moment, the castle door opened. Mordred stepped outside. He raised a megaphone to his mouth. He called, "Atten*tion!*"

The boys snapped up straight and tall.

"Each group leader has a map of part of the Dark Forest," Mordred went on. "Each map shows all the caves in that part. Look in every cave, boys. There's gold in one of them!"

"The Bloodhounds shall find it!" Erica cried.

"Nay!" a boy called out. "The Bulldogs!"

"No! The Wolfhounds!" called another boy.

"Wrong!" another piped up. "The Poodles!"

"That's the spirit, boys!" Mordred cried. He walked down the castle steps. Six skinny DSA student teachers hurried over to him. They carried a large throne-like chair with poles attached to its seat. The student teachers lowered the chair. Mordred sat down in it.

"They're going to *carry* him?" Wiglaf exclaimed.

"You didn't think Uncle Mordred would walk to the Dark Forest, did you?" Angus asked.

"No monkeying around," Mordred called. "I'll come check on you from my camp." He gave a signal. Four student teachers picked up his chair. The others picked up his camping gear. Wiglaf saw that it included pillows, thick blankets, and red pajamas with feet.

Tweeeeeeeeeeeeeeeeet! Mordred gave a blast on his silver whistle. They were off!

Coach led the Bloodhounds across the castle yard. Everyone carried a heavy pack. The

big Marley brothers carried theirs with ease. Wiglaf staggered under his as he marched over the DSA drawbridge.

Wiglaf looked down into the castle moat. How well he remembered Seetha splashing in its waters before she went down for the last time. The secret of where she hid her dragon gold had gone down with her. Now, he was off to hunt for that gold. And, by St. George, he was going to find it!

The Bloodhounds marched up Huntsman's Path. They marched through Vulture Valley. They marched around Leech Lake. And across Swamp River Ridge.

"Halt!" Coach ordered at last.

Wiglaf stopped. There was that lovely word *halt* again. He gladly dropped his pack to the ground.

Coach took out his map. He looked at it for a long time. "We are now in the south part of the Dark Forest," he said. Then he frowned.

He turned the map upside down. "Or are we in the north part?"

Wiglaf and Angus looked over Coach's shoulder.

"Zounds!" Wiglaf cried. "There must be a hundred caves on that map!"

"We'll be marching around here forever!" Angus said. "Let's give up and go home."

"Bloodhounds never give up!" Erica cried.

"That's the way, Eric!" Coach said. "All right, Bloodhounds. On your feet."

The Bloodhounds picked up their packs. They started off. The Marleys marched behind Wiglaf. They began a contest to see which one of them could burp the loudest. Wiglaf thought they all should get first prize.

"Coach?" Erica called out. "I made up a Bloodhound marching song."

"Good work!" Coach cried. "Why don't we sing it as we march?"

Erica sang her song through once. Then all

the Bloodhounds marched through the Dark Forest, singing:

> *"We're the mighty Bloodhounds!*
> *We're dogged and we're bold!*
> *We're the mighty Bloodhounds!*
> *We'll track down Seetha's gold!*
> *We'll put our noses to the ground!*
> *We'll give a mighty sniff!*
> *Will we ever loose the scent?*
> *No! No! Not us! As if!*
> *'Cause...we're the mighty Bloodhounds!*
> *Hear us when we yell!*
> *We're the mighty Bloodhounds!*
> *And do we ever smell!"*

The Bloodhounds looked in twelve caves that morning. Most were empty. But not all. The Cave of Really-Loud-Snoring housed a family of sleeping bears. Cave Hole-in-the-Roof was full of puddles. And Jolly-Good-

Times Cave was piled high with old mead flasks.

Inside Jolly-Good-Times Cave, the Marleys started yelling and whooping and picking up the flasks. They shook them upside down over their mouths. They were hoping for a drop or two of mead, but the flasks were empty.

"Charlie!" cried Coach. "Parley! Whatever your names are! Cut that out!"

He lined everyone up again. Off they marched down Snakes' Path.

"Say, my manly men!" Coach called as they marched. "Who is going to find the gold?"

"The Bloodhounds!" Erica yelled.

Wiglaf hoped Erica was right. That would make all his pain worthwhile. The heavy pack hurt his back. He had blisters on every toe. He was hungry. And it wasn't easy keeping up with Erica.

At a bend in the road, Wiglaf heard a low growl.

"Is that your stomach?" he asked Erica.

"No," she said. "I thought it was yours."

The growling grew louder.

Suddenly a wild man leaped out at them! He had thick white hair. His beard hung down to his knees. He swung a pointed stick over his head and charged at the Blood-hounds!

Chapter 3

Wiglaf ran behind a tree for cover. The Marleys hid behind a big rock. Angus hid behind Wiglaf.

Erica stood her ground beside Coach.

The wild man shook his stick. "Danger!" he cried. "Do not go to the Cave of Doom!"

"Doom?" Wiglaf whispered. "Did he say *doom?*"

"I think so," Angus whispered back. "I'm not going into any cave called Doom."

"Danger!" the hermit cried again. "Do not pass go! Do not stick rocks up your nose!"

"Be gone!" Coach called with a toss of his

head, which made his wig slide to the left.

"First hear my tale!" the hermit cried. "It's a sad tale. Nothing like a fish tail. More like a pig tail. Kind of twisty..."

"Get on with it!" Coach ordered.

"Seven brave men followed me into the Cave of Doom," the hermit said. "We were looking for Seetha's gold!"

"Seetha?" Wiglaf cried. "The dragon?"

"No, Seetha the chipmunk!" The hermit glared at Wiglaf. "Yes, Seetha the dragon. Now, seven men followed me in. But I alone came out alive. Alive, yes. But nutty as a fruitcake. That's why they call me Crazy Looey!"

Wiglaf hoped Looey wasn't both crazy and dangerous. He felt for his lucky rag.

"Oh, we read Seetha's warning," Crazy Looey went on. "But still I led my men deep into the cave. On the cave floor we saw a gold coin. I picked it up. And before you could say, 'The eensy, weensy spider went up the water spout...' " Crazy Looey started making little spider-climbing movements with his fingers.

"Go on, man!" Coach cried. "Go on!"

"Before you could say that," Crazy Looey said, "the cave filled with smoke. Poison smoke! I had set off a booby trap! My seven brave men dropped in their tracks. Dead as ducks. Deader, some of them. Me? I ran. Ran so fast, my hat fell off. It was my best hat, too. The one with a turkey feather—"

"Stop!" Erica called out. "I don't believe a word of this silly story!"

Wiglaf wasn't so sure. True, there was no Cave of Doom on Coach's map. But it sounded like a place Seetha would hide her gold.

"A red-and-white striped turkey feather," Crazy Looey went on. "The prettiest darn feather you ever did see."

"Enough, Cuckoo Looey!" Coach Plungett cried. "Let us pass!"

"That's *Crazy* Looey," the hermit said. "And

I won't let you pass! No way. Not a chance. Never!"

Coach Plungett drew his sword.

"Ah ha!" said Crazy Looey as the tip of Coach's sword touched the tip of his nose. "I see your point!"

The hermit did a little dance. Then he ran away down Snakes' Path, singing: "Down came the rain and washed the spider out...."

The Bloodhounds watched until he disappeared.

Coach put away his sword. "Shame on you for hiding, Bloodhounds!" he said. "You must face danger! Be manly men, like me!"

"Coach?" said Angus. "I don't want to die in the Cave of Doom! I want to go home to DSA! We could make it by sundown."

"Angus, you know Bloodhounds never turn back," Coach scolded. "Now, let's march!"

Wiglaf picked up his pack and started marching. He thought about what Crazy

Looey had said. He didn't mind poking about in caves with old mead flasks. Or even bears, so long as they were asleep. But the Cave of Doom sounded like a very different sort of cave. Wiglaf hoped Crazy Looey had made the whole thing up.

On they marched down Snakes' Path. They passed a large rock. It was shaped like a cow.

The Marley brothers began yelling, "Moo! Moo!"

Erica stopped marching. "Look!" she cried, pointing down at her feet.

Wiglaf looked. Spread across the path in front of him was a giant footprint.

"Is th-that a dragon print?" Angus asked.

"I think so," Erica said. "But we must be sure." She took *The Sir Lancelot Handbook* from her tool belt. She handed it to Wiglaf. "Read me Chapter Two: Are You Sure It's a Dragon Print?"

Wiglaf turned the tiny pages of the book.

At last he found the spot.

"*Dragon prints are big,*" he read. "*Very big.*"

Erica dropped to her knees. She looked at the print through her magnifying glass.

"Yes!" she cried. "This print is very big."

"*A dragon foot has three large toes,*" Wiglaf read. "*So does a dragon print.*"

"One, two, three!" Erica counted. "Yes!"

"*At the tip of each toe will be a deep hole made by a dragon claw,*" he read.

Erica brought her magnifying glass to the tip of the first toe. "Yes!" she cried. She jumped to her feet. "This is a dragon print!"

"Let's get out of here!" Angus howled.

Had this print been made by Seetha? Wiglaf wondered.

Erica called, "Coach! Come here! Quick!"

Coach Plungett hurried back to the spot.

"Egad!" he said when he saw the footprint.

"It's definitely a dragon print, sir," Erica told him.

"And look!" Wiglaf cried. He pointed to the side of the path. "There's another print! And another! They lead into the forest!"

"Put your noses to the ground, Blood-hounds!" cried Coach Plungett. "We shall follow these prints. For as sure as I'm a manly man, they were made by Seetha. And surely they shall lead us to her gold!"

Coach Plungett followed the giant footprints through the Dark Forest. The Bloodhounds followed Coach Plungett.

Wiglaf tried to keep up. But it wasn't easy. Branches scratched his face. Thorns tore at his britches. He had too many blisters to count. And the Marleys were burping again.

Angus turned around. "Here," he said. He handed Wiglaf a stick of his Wild Boar jerky. "This always makes me feel better."

"Thanks," Wiglaf said. But it did not make him feel better. It only made him thirsty.

On the Bloodhounds marched. At last the

dragon prints led to a creek. It was wide and deep. It smelled of dead fish. Thick green ooze lay on top of the water like a blanket. It reminded Wiglaf of something. But he could not think what.

"This is either Clear Water Creek," Coach said. "Or—" he turned the map sideways, "Stinking Green Creek."

Wiglaf had a pretty good idea which creek this was. And now he knew what it reminded him of—his mother's cabbage soup!

Erica took the spyglass from her tool belt. She held it to her eye. "I see dragon prints on the far side of the creek," she told Coach.

"Then we must wade across it," Coach said.

"No!" Angus cried. "Not across *that!*"

The Marleys began to grumble.

"There is no bridge," Coach pointed out. "Wading is the only way. Stop being such babies," he added. "What's a little stinking green ooze to manly men? Now follow me!"

"Sir?" Erica said. "There is another way." Erica took the rope from her tool belt. She threw one end over a tree branch that hung above the creek. Next, she made a loop. She pulled it tight around the branch. Then she knotted the end of the rope.

"Tah dah!" Erica cried. "We can swing across!"

Wiglaf grinned. Back home, he had swung across Pinwick Creek hundreds of times.

"I'll go first," Erica said. She backed up. Her tool belt jangled as she ran for the rope. She jumped on the knot. She swung easily across the creek and hopped off on the far bank.

"Well done!" cried Coach Plungett.

Erica beamed. "Who's next?" she called. She threw the rope over to the other side. Coach caught it. He swung across.

Charlie Marley went next. Then Barley. Then Farley. Harley burped as he swung over.

Harley threw Angus the rope. "Alas, Wiglaf!" Angus whispered. "I'm scared!"

"You can do it," Wiglaf said.

Angus made a few false starts. Then he stood on the knot. Wiglaf pulled the rope back. He gave Angus a mighty push.

Angus sailed over the creek. He landed on the far bank. "Easy as pie!" he exclaimed.

Angus threw Wiglaf the rope. Wiglaf caught it. He backed up. He began to run. He jumped and swung out over the creek.

It was just like swinging over Pinwick Creek—except for one thing. Back home, he never had a great big heavy pack on his back.

Wiglaf felt his fingers slip down the rope.

He lost his hold!

The next thing Wiglaf knew, he was falling toward the slimy green water.

Chapter 4

yiiiiiiiiiiiiiiiiii!" Wiglaf screamed. He splashed down into Stinking Green Creek.

Stinking was right! The water smelled *exactly* like his mother's cabbage soup. Slimy green ooze trickled into Wiglaf's eyes. And his ears. And his mouth. Yuck!

On the bank, the Marleys roared with laughter.

"Wiggie!" Erica called. "Are you all right?"

"Don't swallow!" Angus yelled. "That water will kill you!"

Wiglaf spit out as much ooze as he could. Coach held out a long tree branch. Wiglaf took hold of it. He struggled toward the shore. At last he waded out of the water. He was stinking, green, and oozy.

The Marleys were laughing their heads off.

"Cut it out!" Erica growled at them. "It's not funny." She looked at Wiglaf. She put a hand to her mouth to keep from laughing. "Well, maybe it is. A little."

Angus couldn't help smiling, too.

Great, Wiglaf thought. *Now even my friends are laughing at me!* How he wished this class trip was over.

Wiglaf untied his lucky rag from his sword. He wrung it out. With it he wiped the green slime from his face and arms. He dried his hair. He patted off his clothes.

Coach slapped Wiglaf on the back. "Up and at 'em, now. That's the way. Are you ready to hit the road like a manly man?"

Wiglaf nodded. "Ready," he said. He was

sticky and wet. But he wasn't a quitter. He still wanted to find Seetha's gold.

"Take the lead, Eric," Coach said.

Erica grinned. "Let's march!" she called.

The Bloodhounds marched. They followed the prints onto a road. It was the very road Wiglaf had taken from his home in Pinwick to DSA. Soon the prints led back into the forest again. The afternoon sun dipped low in the sky. And still they followed the dragon prints.

Suddenly Erica stopped. "Coach!" she cried.

"Keep going, Eric," Coach said. "I see more prints over there."

"But we have seen them before!" Erica said. "We are back on Snakes' Path! See? The prints led us in a circle!"

"No jokes!" Angus cried. "I beg of you!"

"Upon my honor, I am not joking," Erica said. "Over there is the rock that looks like a cow. And here is the first print we found!"

Wiglaf saw that Erica was right. "Oh, flea bites!" he cried.

"Alas and alack!" Angus said sadly.

Only the Marleys didn't care. They'd found an anthill and were poking it with sticks.

"How did we *do* that?" Coach said. He took out the map again. He turned it this way and that. Then he pushed back his wig and scratched his hairless head for a long time.

Wiglaf staggered over to the cow-shaped rock. He leaned against it. He felt like crying. He was cold. His feet hurt. He smelled like dead fish. And all for nothing!

Wiglaf slid down against the rock. Then he noticed strange scratch marks on it. He squinted at the rock in the fading light. And he saw that the scratch marks were letters!

"Coach!" Wiglaf cried. "Over here! Hurry!"

Coach Plungett and the other Bloodhounds ran over. Erica lit her mini-torch. Scratched onto the rock by a dragon's claw was:

YOU FOLLOWED MY PRINTS
AND NOW—SURPRISE!
ALL YOU GOT WAS EXERCISE!
YOU'LL NEVER TRACK DOWN
MY HIDING SPOT!
FOR DRAGONS CAN FLY—
AND YOU CANNOT!
SEETHA von FLAMBÉ
P.S. TURN BACK NOW!

"I say we take Seetha's advice!" Angus cried. "Let's turn back *now!*"

"Never!" Erica growled. "Seetha planned to lead us on this wild goose chase before she died. But her mean trick only makes me want to find her gold all the more!"

Wiglaf kicked at the cow-shaped rock. How he wished the Bloodhounds could turn back—just this once.

But Coach had other ideas.

"We shall camp here," he said. "The ground is hard and rocky. But manly men can sleep anywhere!"

The Bloodhounds got out their sleeping bags. Coach began setting up his tent.

In a low voice, Harley Marley called out, "Coach?"

Wiglaf stared. He had heard the Marleys burp. He had heard them laugh and whoop and moo like cows. But this was the first time he had heard any of them speak.

"Yes?" Coach answered. "What is it?"

"We'll set up your tent for you," Harley said. The other Marleys nodded.

Harley and Farley unfolded Coach's tent. Charlie and Barley pounded the tent poles into the ground. Wiglaf and Angus watched, wide-eyed.

At last camp was set up. The Bloodhounds made a fire. Coach passed out sandwiches.

"What *is* this?" Angus asked when he got his. "Hard bread and moldy cheese?"

Coach took a look. "No, you got the *moldy* bread and *hard* cheese sandwich."

Wiglaf pulled his wet sleeping bag close to the fire. He hoped it would dry. Then he stuck his sandwich on a stick. He toasted it over the campfire. It didn't make it taste any better. But at least it was warm going down.

Erica poured cider into her collapsible goblet. The rest of the Bloodhounds took turns drinking from the jug. Wiglaf hoped it was not the jug that had been home to Sir Mort's false teeth.

"Into your sleeping bags, Bloodhounds," Coach said after supper. "I am going to tell you a ghost story."

Wiglaf slid into his sleeping bag. It still smelled of fish. But it was almost dry.

"Once there lived an executioner," Coach began. "Every night at twelve o'clock, he took his axe and chopped off someone's head. He always wore a black hood. So no one knew what he looked like."

"Coach!" cried Angus. "This is too scary!"

"Oh, stop up your ears, Angus," Erica snapped. "The rest of us want to hear this."

Wiglaf wasn't so sure. A story about beheading was likely to be bloody. And Wiglaf's stomach turned over if he even thought about blood.

"The executioner," Coach continued, "walked through the Dark Forest with his axe. And as he went, he sang this song:

"If ever you hear me walking by,
*It may be **you** who's the next to die!*
I'll lay your neck on a chopping block,
And whack off your head at twelve o'clock!
I'll wrap you up in a big white sheet,
And bury you down six feet deep!
Then the worms crawl in! And the worms crawl out!

They'll eat your guts and then spit them out!
They'll peel your skin! They'll drink your blood!
Till all that's left are your bones in the mud!"

Wiglaf was about to stick his fingers in his ears. He didn't want to hear another word! But Coach went on with his tale. "The executioner chopped off hundreds and hundreds of heads. And then one day, it happened."

"What happened?" asked Erica.

"The executioner swung his axe too hard," Coach said. "And he chopped off his own bloody head!"

Uck! Wiglaf hoped he wouldn't be sick!

"The executioner's head rolled down a hill," Coach went on. "It splashed into Bottomless Lake and sank to the bottom."

"I'm glad he's dead!" Angus cried.

"Oh, he's dead, all right," Coach said. "But now his ghost walks through the Dark Forest.

He's looking for heads to chop off. For, you see, he needs a new head."

Angus began whimpering with fear.

Wiglaf held tight to his lucky rag.

"Now every night at midnight," Coach went on, "the ghost sings his song. So be careful in the Dark Forest, boys. If you hear someone singing: 'The worms crawl in, the worms crawl out...' Beware! It's the headless executioner, coming after *you!*"

Chapter 5

’m afraid to sleep," Angus whispered.

"Scaredy-cat!" Erica laughed. But Wiglaf thought that even her voice sounded shaky.

"Maybe it's not *this* Dark Forest," Angus said. "Maybe it's some *other* Dark Forest."

"Maybe," Wiglaf said. But as far as he knew there was only one Dark Forest.

Wiglaf heard a hissing sound. And another! He sat up in his sleeping bag. His heart was pounding. But it was only the Marleys. They were taking turns spitting into the campfire.

"Coach, I can't go to sleep," Angus said. "I'm afraid the ghost will come."

"Piffle!" Coach said. "I told you that story to make you brave. I want you to grow up to be a big, strong, manly man—like me!" He stood up. "I am going to my tent," he said. "Sleep well!"

"Good night, Coach!" Erica called.

"Sweet dreams!" called Harley Marley.

Then all the Marleys started laughing.

What is their problem? Wiglaf wondered.

Coach ducked into his tent. He closed the tent flap behind him. Wiglaf heard him humming a marching song as he got ready for bed.

Wiglaf closed his eyes. He heard owls calling. He heard crickets singing. He heard a Marley hocking something up from deep in his throat. He heard a horrible, bloodcurdling scream. Wiglaf's eyes popped open.

Suddenly Coach shot out of his tent. He held his sleeping bag tightly around him. He jumped around, screaming.

"The executioner's after him!" Angus cried. He disappeared into his sleeping bag.

"Help!" Coach screamed. "Don't let them get me!"

The Marleys rolled on the ground, laughing.

Coach kept jumping around. Then—*BONK!* He hit his head on a low tree branch. His nightcap and his wig stuck on the branch. But the rest of him fell to the ground.

Wiglaf jumped up. He forgot his own fear as he ran to his fallen leader.

"Coach?" Wiglaf cried. "Can you hear me?"

Coach didn't answer. He was out cold.

Erica reached Coach next. She patted his face. "Wake up, Coach!" she said.

The Marleys kept laughing and snorting.

At last Angus crawled out of his sleeping bag. He made his way slowly over to Coach. He poked him with his toe.

But Coach didn't move. Not even when

Wiglaf put his wig back on his head.

"What could have undone him so?" Erica asked. As if in answer, a sound came from inside Coach's tent: *Ribbit! Ribbit!*

Wiglaf and the others saw a dozen little frogs hop out of the tent. *Ribbit!* they croaked as they hopped away.

The Marleys laughed even harder.

Suddenly Wiglaf understood. No wonder the Marleys had been so helpful. They had planted the frogs inside Coach's tent!

"For a manly man," Angus said, "Coach sure is scared of frogs."

Erica splashed Coach with cold water from her canteen. At last Coach opened his eyes. He sat up. He smiled a strange smile.

"Hallo!" he said. "And who are you, young lads?"

"The Bloodhounds," Erica answered.

"You don't look like doggies!" Coach giggled.

"Uh-oh," said Angus.

"Coach?" Erica said. "Do you know your name?"

The silly smile appeared on Coach's face once more. "Is it...Rumpelstiltskin?"

"Guess again," Erica said.

"I know!" Coach exclaimed. "I'm Queen Mary!"

"He needs help," Erica said. "But nothing on my tool belt is going to do the trick."

"We have to get him to DSA," Wiglaf said.

"I'll take him!" Angus cried. He jumped up. "I'll do anything to get out of this forest!"

But Harley spoke up. "We'll take him," he said. His brothers nodded.

Wiglaf didn't think this was a very good idea. But he was not about to argue with the four big brothers.

Barley and Charlie held onto each other's arms, making a seat. Coach wobbled over and sat down on it. The Marleys lifted him up.

And they started off for DSA.

"Farewell from the queen!" Coach called. He blew kisses. Then he began to sing. "Queen Mary had a little lamb! Little lamb! Little lamb! Queen Mary had a little lamb! Its fleece was white as cheese!"

"All right, Bloodhounds!" Erica said to the two who were left. "It's just us now. We must find Seetha's gold for good old Coach Plungett! We shall make him proud of us. Because who is the best?"

"Who?" asked Angus.

"The Bloodhounds!" Erica cried.

The three of them pulled their sleeping bags into Coach's tent. They lined them up close together and crawled inside.

Wiglaf untied his lucky rag from his sword. He held it tightly and closed his eyes. He tried counting unicorns. After some two hundred, he finally fell asleep.

In the middle of the night, Wiglaf sat up

with a start. What had woken him? He listened. He heard a strange high voice, singing.

The little hairs on the back of Wiglaf's neck stood up. He squeezed his lucky rag. *Don't let it be the executioner's ghost!* he said over and over to himself.

The singing grew louder. The singer was coming closer!

"Does anybody hear singing?" Wiglaf whispered.

"Singing huh?" Angus said, waking up.

"I hear it," Erica said. She sounded scared.

The voice grew louder still.

Now they all heard what it was singing: *"Then the worms crawl in! And the worms crawl out! They'll eat your guts and then spit them out!"*

Angus gasped. "It's the executioner!"

Wiglaf slid out of his sleeping bag. He tiptoed over to the tent flap. He peeked outside. He didn't see a thing. But he heard the high voice more clearly now: *"They'll peel your skin!*

They'll drink your blood! Till all that's left are your bones in the mud!"

Erica began rattling the tools on her belt. "There must be something here I can use to make a ghost go away," she whispered.

Angus crawled over to Wiglaf. He, too, peeked out of the tent.

"There it is!" he whispered. He pointed with a shaky hand.

Wiglaf saw a shadowy shape.

"That can't be the executioner's ghost," Wiglaf told Angus. "It's too short."

"You'd be short, too, if you didn't have a head," Erica pointed out. "Call to it, Wiggie. Speak bravely. Maybe it won't harm us."

"Who...who...who goes there?" he said at last.

"Me!" called the shape.

"Me who?" Wiglaf called back.

"Me, Dudwin!"

Wiglaf gasped. He stuck his head out of the tent. "Dudwin?" he exclaimed. "Dudwin of Pinwick?"

"That's the one," the voice replied.

"Who is it, Wiglaf?" asked Erica. "What's going on?"

"Has he come to chop off our heads?" Angus whispered.

"It's not the ghost," Wiglaf said. "It's my little brother, Dudwin!"

Chapter 6

Wiglaf dashed out of the tent. He ran until he reached a sturdy boy of seven.

"Dudwin! It *is* you!" Wiglaf exclaimed. He saw that Dudwin had grown. And now—alas! His little brother was taller than he was!

Erica lit her mini-torch. She shone it on Wiglaf's brother. The boy had a round face and thick yellow hair. His tunic fit snugly over his belly. He wore baggy brown britches.

"Hallo, Wiggie!" Dudwin grinned. One front tooth was missing. He opened his arms and hugged Wiglaf—hard.

"Dudwin!" Wiglaf cried. "Let go!"

Dudwin did. "You smell like fish, Wiggie."

"What are you doing here, Dud?" Wiglaf asked, quickly changing the subject.

"I was on my way to your school," Dudwin explained. "Father sent me. He wants me to bring him all the gold you've got so far."

"Oh, great!" Wiglaf said under his breath.

"Dudwin," said Erica. "Why were you singing that worm song?"

"I like that song," Dudwin said. "Another one I like is 'Greasy, Grimy Gopher Guts.' Oh, and speaking of greasy..." Dudwin took a large flask from his pack. "Mother sent you some of her cabbage soup."

"Egad!" Wiglaf exclaimed. "I hoped never to taste that soup again as long as I live!"

"I love cabbage soup!" Angus cried. "If you don't want it, I'll take it!" He grabbed the flask from Dudwin. He popped the cork. He took a sniff. "Eeeeeew!" he cried. "Wiglaf! Is your own mother trying to poison you?"

"Sometimes I wonder," Wiglaf said. "But it

was kind of her to send it." He took the flask, put the cork back in place, and handed it to his brother. "Hold onto it for me, Dud."

They walked back to camp. The sun was coming up, so there was no use trying to sleep now. Erica rubbed two dry sticks together and lit a fire. They all sat around it, warming their cold hands. Wiglaf wished that he did not have to give his brother bad news.

"Dudwin," he said at last, "you must go home empty-handed. I have no gold yet."

Dudwin frowned. "Father won't like that."

"No. But he will like this," Wiglaf said. "Tell him that *I* am a dragon slayer!"

"Oh, right!" Dudwin laughed loudly. He slapped Wiglaf on the back—hard. "Tell me another one, Wiggie!"

"Two dragons have died by my hand," Wiglaf said. "Well, more or less, by my hand."

"Aw, go on!" Dudwin shot back.

"It's true," Angus put in.

"For real?" Dudwin asked Erica.

Erica nodded. "I helped him, of course."

"But Wiggie hates the sight of blood," Dudwin said. "Back home, he wouldn't even swat a fly. Once he cut his thumb and fainted. He never—"

"Never mind!" Wiglaf cut in. "You must go home after breakfast, Dudwin. Tell Father that when I have gold, I shall bring it myself."

"But Father thinks I'll be gone for a week," Dudwin said. "I don't want to go home yet!"

"You must," Wiglaf said. "We are hunting dragon treasure. You would be in the way."

"No, I wouldn't!" Dudwin cried. "I can help you! I'm good at finding treasure. I found lots on my way here." He emptied his pockets. "Look!" he said. "I found a diamond!"

"That's a sparkly rock, Dudwin," Wiglaf said.

Dudwin ignored his brother. "Here is a spur from the boot of a knight!" he went on.

"That's nothing but a piece of a pinecone!" Wiglaf said.

"And here is the best treasure of all," the boy said happily. "The tip of a wizard's wand!"

"That, Dudwin," Wiglaf growled, "is a twig!"

"Lighten up, Wiglaf," Erica said with a laugh. "Dudwin has some fine treasures."

Dudwin grinned. "Yeah. Lighten up, Wiggie."

Wiglaf rolled his eyes.

"Let him stay, Wiglaf," Angus added. "Dudwin can be an honorary Bloodhound."

"Oh, boy!" Dudwin cried.

"We shall soon find Seetha's gold," Erica pointed out. "And Dudwin can take some straight home to your father."

"Yes, yes!" Dudwin cried.

"Four is better than three," Angus said. "Dudwin can help us carry our gear."

This last point won Wiglaf over. "All right, Dudwin," he told his brother. "You can stay."

Dudwin grinned. "I was going to anyway, Wiggie," he said.

After breakfast, Erica called, "Bloodhounds, march!"

"Wait!" Dudwin cried. "I see a goblin's hat!" He ran off and picked up an acorn cap.

Erica tapped her foot and waited for him to come back. Then off they went.

Wiglaf marched behind Dudwin. Deep down, he felt glad that his brother was with them. True, Dudwin could be a pain. But he had his good points. After all, he was carrying a heavy pack. And this meant Wiglaf's own pack was lighter.

That morning, the Bloodhounds hunted for Seetha's treasure in Bats-a-Plenty Cave. They searched Chock-Full-of-Spiders Cave. And Leeches-R-Us Cave. They looked for treasure in cave after cave. But they came out of each one empty-handed.

Except for Dudwin.

"Oh, boy!" he cried, sliding out of Slippery Cave. "I found a baby dragon's tooth!"

"That's a pebble, Dud," Wiglaf said.

"Here is a fine treasure!" Dudwin called inside Slimy Cave. "A goblet fit for a king!"

"Dudwin!" Erica cried. "You took that from my tool belt!" She grabbed her goblet back.

Erica marched the Bloodhounds from cave to cave. The day grew hot. The Bloodhounds began to sweat. Mosquitoes bit them.

As they started over the Shiver River Bridge, Angus called, "Let's stop for a swim!"

"Bloodhounds never stop!" Erica said.

But halfway across the bridge, Erica stopped. And Wiglaf saw why.

A great hairy arm, waving a big spiked club, was sticking up from under the bridge.

"Yikes!" Angus cried. "It's a troll!"

"Right!" the troll roared. He pulled himself up onto the bridge. "And this is my bridge!"

The troll's eyes darted from face to face. "Who wants me to eat them first?" he roared.

No Bloodhound volunteered. Not even Erica.

"Someone step forward!" cried the troll. "If I eat you all at once, I'll get a bellyache!"

No Bloodhound stepped forward.

"You are one ugly troll!" Dudwin shouted.

"Shush, Dudwin!" Wiglaf clapped a hand over his brother's mouth.

Erica drew her sword. "Back off, troll!"

"Make me!" the troll cried. He swung his club and knocked Erica's sword into the river.

"Alas!" Erica cried. "That was my special Sir Lancelot look-alike sword!"

The troll laughed. He reached out a long arm, snatched up Angus, and dangled him over his mouth.

"No! Don't eat me!" Angus cried. "I'll give you a *bad* bellyache!"

"Hey, Troll-breath!" Dudwin yelled.

"Dudwin, stop it!" Wiglaf cried.

Dudwin paid no attention. "I have something much yummier than him!" he shouted.

"What?" the troll growled.

"Cabbage soup," Dudwin answered.

The troll eyed Dudwin. "Homemade?" he asked.

Dudwin nodded. "By my own mother."

"Give it here," said the troll.

Dudwin pulled the flask from his pack.

"Don't, Dudwin!" Wiglaf begged. "Mother's soup will make him *really* mad!"

But Dudwin stepped bravely up to the troll. He popped the cork off the flask. A sickening smell filled the air. Dudwin quickly splashed the soup in the troll's face.

The troll's eyes grew wide with surprise. He stuck out his tongue and licked some of the soup from his face. "Mmmmmmm!" he growled.

Wiglaf gasped. "You like it?" he cried.

"Like it?" said the troll. "I love it!" He dropped Angus onto the bridge. "I'll eat you humans later. Now, I want more soup!"

"You got it!" Dudwin said. He threw the flask to the troll.

While the troll gulped down the soup, the Bloodhounds ran across his bridge. They kept running until the troll was far behind. Then they fell down, gasping for breath.

"Nice work, Dudwin!" Erica exclaimed.

"*Very* nice," Angus said. "How is it that you were brave enough to stand up to the troll?"

"Oh, all my brothers are much meaner than the troll," Dudwin said. "Except for Wiglaf."

Wiglaf patted his brother on the back. He was proud of Dudwin. But at the same time, he felt—well, ashamed. His little brother was taller than he was. His little brother carried a bigger pack. And now his little brother had saved them from the troll. It was hard to take.

While Angus rested after his near-death-by-troll experience, Dudwin ran off. He was gone for a long time. Wiglaf was starting to worry when he came running back.

"Eric!" Dudwin cried. "Look what I found!"

"Shhh," Erica said. "I'm checking the map."

Dudwin ran over to Angus. "Look at this!" he exclaimed.

"Don't bother me, Dudwin," Angus said. "Not after what I've been through."

Dudwin turned to his brother. "Wiggie?"

Wiglaf sighed. "What did you find, Dud?"

Dudwin held out his hand to Wiglaf.

"Egad!" cried Wiglaf.

For there in Dudwin's grubby hand lay two golden coins.

Chapter 7

old coins!" Wiglaf cried. "Where did you find them, Dudwin?"

"Gold?" Erica exclaimed. "Did you say *gold*?" She and Angus hurried over.

"I found them—" Dudwin began eagerly. Then he stopped. A strange look came over his face. "I'm not telling," he said.

"What?" Erica cried. "Why not?"

"Because," Dudwin said, "you keep making fun of my treasure."

"Don't be that way, Dudwin," Erica said. "Seetha must have dropped the coins on her way to her secret hiding place. Show us where you found them. The Cave of Doom will be close by. Come on, Dudwin!"

But Dudwin only shook his head *no*.

Erica pulled Wiglaf and Angus aside. "He's *your* brother, Wiglaf," Erica said in a low voice so Dudwin couldn't hear. "Make him tell!"

Wiglaf rolled his eyes. "What do you want me to do? Torture him?"

"If that's what it takes," Erica shot back.

Wiglaf really wanted to find the gold. If he did, he wouldn't have to send Dudwin home empty-handed. And he was sure Mordred would stop picking on him. He had to get Dudwin to tell where he found the coins so they could find the cave. He thought hard.

"Dudwin is stubborn," he told Erica at last. "Talking to him will do no good. But try offering him something from your tool belt."

Erica gasped. "I saved up for six months to buy this tool belt! Why should I be the one to bribe Dudwin?"

"Because you are the only one with any-thing to trade," Angus pointed out.

They walked back over to Dudwin.

"Dudwin," Erica said, "show us where you found the coins. If you do, I shall give you a tool from my Sir Lancelot Tool Belt."

"Oh, boy!" Dudwin cried. "Which one?"

"Well..." Erica said. "The toothpick."

Dudwin shook his head.

"The lice comb?"

"No way," Dudwin said.

Erica sighed. "What do you want?"

Dudwin grinned. "The torch."

"What?" Erica cried. "That is my best tool!"

Dudwin jingled the coins in his pocket.

Erica took the torch from her belt. She looked at it longingly. Then she handed it to Dudwin.

"Oh, boy!" Dudwin exclaimed. "Now I can find treasures in the dark!"

"Cut the chitchat," Erica snapped. "Show us where you found the coins."

Dudwin led the way through the forest. He stopped at the foot of a big hill, covered with vines. "There," he said.

"Clear the brush, Bloodhounds!" Erica ordered. "Keep a lookout for coins!"

Wiglaf and Angus drew their swords. They began hacking away at the vines. But they found that the vines were not really growing on the hill. They had only been piled up there as if to hide something. The boys pulled the vines away and discovered a great hole in the side of the hill.

"It's the mouth of a cave!" cried Angus.

Wiglaf's eyes grew wide. Pointed rocks hung down over the cave entrance. It looked exactly like the open mouth of a dragon!

A wooden sign had fallen face down beside the entrance. Wiglaf picked it up. It said:

WELCOME TO
THE CAVE OF DOOM!

Wiglaf quickly dropped the sign. They had found the Cave of Doom!

"Footprints!" Erica cried suddenly. "Going into the cave!" She studied the prints with her magnifying glass. "They're Seetha's, all right," she said. "I'm going in. Who's going with me?"

"Not me," said Angus.

"Me!" cried Dudwin.

"No, Dud," Wiglaf said. "You stay out here with Angus. I—I'll go in."

"But it's dark in the cave." Dudwin held up the torch. "And I have the light."

"Good point," Erica said. "And very brave of you to want to come." She shot Angus a look.

"Oh, all right," Angus said. "I'll come, too."

"All right, Bloodhounds," Erica said. "Let's go in!"

"Not so fast!" called a voice behind them. "Not so fast!"

Wiglaf whirled around. There, sitting on his throne-like chair, was Mordred!

"Greetings, Bloodhounds!" Mordred smiled at them. None of the skinny student teachers were smiling. They were struggling to put their heavy headmaster down gently.

"I have come to see how you are doing," Mordred said. "Where is Plungett?"

"He had an accident, Uncle," Angus said. "The Marley brothers took him back to DSA."

"Egad!" Mordred cried. "I hope he is not hurt badly. It would not be easy to find a new slaying coach. Not at the salary I pay." His violet eyes lit upon Dudwin. "And who, pray tell, is *this?*"

"Dudwin," Wiglaf answered. "My brother."

"Why in the name of King Ken's britches is your big brother here?" Mordred barked.

"He's my *little* brother," Wiglaf said. "But, sir! We have found Seetha's hiding spot. Somewhere inside this cave is her gold."

Wiglaf had said the magic word: gold.

Mordred jumped down from his chair. "Oh, joy!" he cried. "Oh, happy day! Come! I shall lead you into the cave myself!"

Mordred took a step toward the dark mouth of the cave. Then he stopped.

"On second thought," he said, "I shall *follow* you Bloodhounds into the cave. That way I can make sure nothing sneaks up on you from behind." Mordred pointed at Dudwin. "You with the torch!" he said. "Lead the way!"

"To the treasure!" Dudwin yelled. And he ran into the cave.

Wiglaf, Erica, and Angus hurried after him. The torchlight threw tall shadows onto the stony walls. High above Wiglaf's head long, thin stalactites hung down from the ceiling. There were hundreds of them. They looked like stone fangs!

"Don't dawdle!" Mordred called from behind. "Do you see any sign of the gold?"

"Not yet, sir!" Erica called back.

Suddenly Dudwin tripped. The torch flew from his hand as he fell.

Wiglaf reached down to help him up. As he picked up the torch, he saw that his brother had fallen over a pile of white shapes. It took him a moment to understand what they were.

"B-b-b-bones!" Wiglaf cried.

"Bones?" Angus screamed. He took off for the mouth of the cave.

"Oof!" Mordred grunted as his nephew ran into him. He grabbed Angus's arm.

"Let go!" Angus cried. "I'm out of here!"

"Are you mad?" Mordred roared. "We're so close to Seetha's gold, I can almost smell it!"

"I think that smell is dried bat droppings, sir," Erica offered.

"Whatever," Mordred said. He turned Angus around. "Onward!"

"Whose bones are they, Wiggie?" Dudwin asked as they began inching forward.

"Some big animal probably died here long ago," Wiglaf said. He hoped it was true.

"I want to keep some," Dudwin said. He began picking up bones.

"What's the holdup?" Mordred yelled from the back of the line. "Go! Go! Go!"

"What's this?" Erica said. She bent down. But instead of a bone, she picked up a hat.

Wiglaf stared at the thing in Erica's hand. "What is stuck in that hat?" he asked.

"Looks like a red-and-white striped turkey feather," Erica answered. "And it is the prettiest darn feather I ever did see."

"This must be Crazy Looey's hat!" Wiglaf

cried. "And these bones! They must be the bones of his seven brave men!"

"Move!" Mordred called. "Moooove!"

"We are doomed!" Angus howled.

"I'm too young to get doomed!" Dudwin cried. The torchlight wavered as his hand began to shake. "I want to go back, Wiggie!"

"Be brave, Dudwin," Wiglaf whispered. "You are a Bloodhound now. And Bloodhounds never turn back. Besides," he added, "Mordred won't let you turn back."

Wiglaf untied his lucky rag from his sword.

"Here, Dudwin," he said, handing it to him. "This has always brought me luck. I am sure it will keep you from being doomed."

"Thanks, Wiggie." Dudwin sniffed. He held the rag tightly as he began walking again.

Erica started singing in a shaky voice: *"We're the mighty Bloodhounds...We're dogged and we're bold..."*

The others joined in. Their voices echoed as they walked toward a faint yellow glow far back in the cave. They followed Dudwin through a passageway. They came out in a big open space lit by a strange, yellow light.

Wiglaf blinked. And then he saw before him a life-sized statue of Seetha! Her wings were spread. Her tail was curled around a giant stone bowl. And piled high in the bowl were bright, shining golden coins!

Mordred pushed past Wiglaf. "Gold!" he cried. Tears of joy sprang to his eyes. "A mountain of gold! And it all belongs to ME!"

Chapter 8

on't start counting your gold yet, sir!"
Wiglaf said. "Look! Seetha has left us a
message on the wall!" And he began to read
what had been scratched in stone:

If I die, I, Seetha von Flambé, leave all my
gold to my 3,683 children. To anyone else
who finds my gold—anyone who is NOT one
of my beautiful children—I leave this warning:

GO AWAY! GO FAR AWAY!
DO NOT COME BACK SOME OTHER DAY!
FOR IF YOU STEAL A COIN—JUST ONE...
YOU'LL MEET YOUR DOOM—

IT WON'T BE FUN.
SMOKE WILL CHOKE YOU!
FIRES WILL BLAZE!
THE CAVE WILL SHAKE!
YOU'LL BE AMAZED!
SPEARS SHALL RAIN DOWN FROM ON HIGH!
AND <u>YOU</u> SHALL BE THE NEXT TO DIE!

"I'm scared!" Dudwin cried.

"Me, too!" Angus said.

Wiglaf started shaking.

Even Erica looked scared.

"Don't be such sausages!" Mordred cried. "What else would a dragon say? 'Go ahead. Help yourself to all my gold!' I don't think so!"

"Please Uncle Mordred!" Angus fell to his knees. "Let's get out of here! I beg you! Seetha may be dead. But she means business!"

"Fiddlesticks!" Mordred barked. "Stop stalling, all of you! Go get my gold!"

Then, to Wiglaf's horror, Dudwin spoke up. "You're the one who wants the gold," he told Mordred. "So why don't you get it yourself?"

"What?" roared Mordred. "Me? Don't you know why boys were invented? So grown-ups never have to do anything they don't want to! Now, *go get my gold!*"

The Bloodhounds stayed close together. They inched toward the bowl of treasure.

"Okay," said Erica when they reached it. "Who shall take the first coin from the pile?"

Wiglaf swallowed. Here was a chance for him to do a brave deed. Besides, if taking a coin set off a booby trap, what did it matter who took it? They were all goners.

"I'll do it," Wiglaf said. He drew a breath. Slowly he slid a coin from the pile. He waited for the smoke and fire.

But nothing happened.

Mordred cried, "What did I tell you, boys? Seetha's warning was pure poppycock!"

Then Wiglaf heard a low rumble.

"Is that your stomach?" he asked Erica.

"No," she said. "I thought it was yours."

The rumbling grew louder.

"Ohhh!" howled Angus. "It's doom time!"

Wiglaf swallowed. He quickly tossed the coin back onto the pile of gold.

Too late!

The rumbling thundered louder. Then the gold in the big stone bowl started to spin around and around. It quickly picked up speed. The coins circled the bowl faster and faster. Then, as if someone had pulled a plug at the bottom of the bowl, the coins began to disappear down a hole. *SLUUUUUURP!*

"What's happening?" Mordred cried.

"The gold is going down some kind of drain!" Angus answered.

"WHAT?" Mordred screamed. And he started running toward the stone dragon.

The Bloodhounds jumped out of the way as the headmaster took a flying leap into the bowl. He slid down, grabbing for the coins.

There was a final *SLURP!* Then it was still.

"All is not lost!" Mordred cried happily. "I have a great big handful of gold!"

Mordred tried to pull his arm out. But his fist, full of coins, was stuck in the hole.

"Help me, lads!" Mordred cried.

The Bloodhounds held onto Mordred's boots. They pulled with all their might. At last...*POP!* Off came the boots.

"You ninnies!" Mordred cried. "Pull *me!*"

The Bloodhounds grabbed Mordred's feet. They pulled as hard as they could. But his fist stayed stuck.

"Stop," Mordred cried at last. "Leave me here, boys. Carry on at DSA as best you can without me. It won't be easy. But you must try!"

"But Uncle Mor—" Angus began.

"No, nephew," Mordred said. "Do not try to comfort me. My death will be slow. Slow and very terrible. But I shall be brave and—"

"Sir?" Erica cut in.

"Quiet!" Mordred snapped. "As I was saying, I shall be brave. And so it is fitting that one of the DSA towers be named for me. The north one, I think. Mordred's Tower. That has a nice ring to it."

"You don't have to die here, sir!" Wiglaf said. "You *can* save yourself!"

"Blazing King Ken's britches!" Mordred cried. "Are you going to pester me to death? Well, tell me, boy. How can I save myself?"

And Wiglaf said, "Let go of the gold."

"Let go?" Mordred looked puzzled.

"Yes, Uncle!" Angus answered. "Then your hand can slide out of the hole."

Mordred frowned. "You cannot mean I should give up the gold? No. Never."

Wiglaf turned to Erica. "We have to get out of here!" he said. "What shall we do?"

"I don't know," Erica said. "But Sir Lancelot will." She yanked *The Sir Lancelot Handbook* from her belt. She began turning pages. "Ah ha!" she cried happily. "Here, under 'Emergencies.'" She began to read aloud: *"Emergency #54: Is there a great big greedy man whose hand is stuck down a hole because he won't let go of a fist full of gold coins?"*

"Yes!" cried Angus. "Yes! That's it exactly!"

"If the great big greedy man doesn't hurry up and let go," Erica read on, *"are you in danger of being doomed?"*

"Yes!" Angus cried. "Right again!"

Erica read on. *"When all else fails..."* She turned the page. *"...try tickling!"*

"Oh, boy!" Dudwin cried.

Then all four Bloodhounds jumped on Mordred.

"Stop!" cried Mordred. "What are you doing?"

"Sorry, sir," Erica said. She was tickling his belly. "But it's for your own good."

"Hoo-hoo!" Mordred howled. "Oh! Stop!"

No one stopped. Angus tickled Mordred's left foot. Wiglaf did the same to his right. Dudwin chucked him under the chin.

Mordred wiggled and giggled. He kicked and screamed, "Have mercy!"

But the Bloodhounds kept on. At last Wiglaf heard *Clink! Clink! Clink!* as the coins fell from Mordred's fist.

"It worked!" he cried.

"Of course it did!" Erica exclaimed. "Sir Lancelot has never let me down!"

"Noooo!" Mordred sobbed as his hand—his empty hand—popped out of the hole. He pushed away the ticklers. His eyes glowed with red-hot fury.

"Trick *me* out of my gold, will you?" he cried. He pulled on his boots. "Wait till I get my hands on you!"

"But, sir!" Erica said. "We couldn't leave you here to die!"

"Don't argue with him!" Wiglaf said. "Let's go!"

"Wait!" Dudwin yelled. "I spy treasure!"

"Treasure?" Mordred cried. "Where?"

Dudwin pushed the torch into Wiglaf's hand. Then he started climbing up the dragon statue.

"Stop!" Wiglaf cried. "Dudwin! Come back down!"

But Dudwin kept climbing. And now Wiglaf saw why. Between its stone teeth, the dragon statue held one last gold coin.

Mordred's eyes lit up as he saw it, too. He lunged for the statue.

"There is just one coin, boy!" the headmaster roared. "Just one! And it's mine!"

One coin. Just one. Seetha's warning rang inside Wiglaf's head.

FOR IF YOU STEAL A COIN—JUST ONE...
YOU'LL MEET YOUR DOOM—
IT WON'T BE FUN.

Now Wiglaf understood. Seetha's warning was about one coin—just one! And suddenly he knew that the warning wasn't poppycock at all.

"Don't touch that coin!" Wiglaf yelled to the climbers. "Don't touch it!"

Too late! Mordred had already snatched the coin from between the dragon's teeth.

"Ha ha!" he cried. "I got it first! I got—"

Mordred got no further.

A flame shot from the statue's mouth.

"Yowie!" Mordred cried. He jumped down.

Dudwin jumped down, too.

Smoke began to pour from the stone dragon's nose. More flames shot from between its jaws. The cave walls began to shake.

THWUNK! A stalactite dropped from the ceiling.

Wiglaf stared at the quivering stone spear in front of him. It had missed him by inches!

THWUNK! Another dropped beside him.

THWUNK! And another!

And then, just as Seetha had warned, hundreds of stone spears began raining down.

"Help!" cried Angus. "We're doomed!"

Chapter 9

Wiglaf grabbed Dudwin's hand. He ran through the smoke, pulling his brother with him.

THWUNK! A stalactite landed right behind them.

Wiglaf dropped the torch. It hit the cave floor and sputtered out. The cave was dark now. And filled with smoke. Wiglaf could hardly breathe. But he kept going. Far off, he thought he saw light. The mouth of the cave!

THWUNK!

Wiglaf jumped back from the stalactite. Dudwin's hand slid out of his.

THWUNK! THWUNK! THWUNK!

Stone spears were falling thick and fast! Wiglaf ran for his life. He thought his brother was ahead of him. "Run toward the light, Dudwin!" he yelled.

Wiglaf heard a *whoosh* as Mordred raced by him.

At last, Wiglaf reached the mouth of the cave. He ran out into the daylight, gasping for air.

He saw Erica. And Mordred was leaning against the student teachers, catching his breath. But where was Dudwin?

Wiglaf heard footsteps. That had to be his brother. But a second later, Angus ran out of the cave.

"I'm not doomed after all!" Angus cried.

Wiglaf ran back to the mouth of the cave. "Dudwin?" he called. "Are you in there?"

"I'm stuck!" came the faint reply. "Help me, Wiggie!"

"I'm coming!" Wiglaf raced back into the cave. Falling stalactites whistled by him.

"Over here, Wiggie!" the boy cried.

Wiglaf turned toward the voice. At last he found his brother. A stalactite had stabbed through Dudwin's baggy britches, pinning him to the spot.

Wiglaf tugged on the stalactite. He pulled with all his might. But it stayed stuck.

"Step out of your breeches, Dud," Wiglaf said. "Hurry! You'll have to leave them here."

"No way!" Dudwin cried. "My treasures are in my pockets."

Wiglaf groaned. He didn't have time to argue. He felt like giving his stubborn little brother a kick in the shin. Instead, he drew back his foot and kicked the stalactite—hard!

Snap! It broke off at the base.

"Oooh!" Wiglaf cried. Had he broken all his toes, too?

"Way to go, Wiggie!" cried Dudwin.

Wiglaf grabbed Dudwin again. He forgot about his throbbing toes as he pulled his brother toward the light.

Then, to his horror, he saw that stone spears were falling right inside the mouth of the cave. And falling fast! The entrance was almost blocked!

"Faster, Dud!" Wiglaf cried. "Faster!" Wiglaf pushed Dudwin—hard! His brother half flew out of the cave.

Wiglaf dove after him. He rolled away as the spears filled the mouth of the cave. He lay on the ground, panting.

Dudwin raced over to Wiglaf. He helped him up. He threw his arms around him.

"Wiglaf!" he cried. "You saved my life!"

"Pipe down, you blasted boys!" Mordred yelled. "If not for you, I'd be a rich man!"

"A rich *dead* man," Angus added.

Dudwin ran over to Mordred. "I want to be

like my brave big brother! I want to go to Dragon Slayers' Academy. Can I? Please?"

"You must be joking!" Mordred cried. "Wiglaf still owes me his seven pennies. You think I would let his brother in for free?"

"I can pay!" Dudwin said. He reached into his pocket. He pulled out his two gold coins.

Mordred's eyes almost popped out of his head. "Those are *my* coins!" he roared. "I dropped them! Right in the spot where you found them!"

Dudwin pulled his hand back. "I'm not falling for *that* old trick!"

"Give him one coin, Dud," Wiglaf whispered. "Or you shall lose both of them."

"If you say so, Wiglaf," Dudwin said.

And he threw one coin in a bush.

Mordred dove after it.

"Now run home with the other coin," Wiglaf said. "Quickly, Dud! Before Mordred tries to get his hands on it!"

Dudwin slipped the coin into his pocket. He picked up his pack. He gave Wiglaf back his lucky rag. "It worked, Wiggie," Dudwin said. "I didn't get doomed."

"Farewell, Dudwin!" Wiglaf said.

"Goodbye, Wiggie!" Dudwin smiled. "I'll tell them at home how you saved my life in the Cave of Doom! I'll tell them you are a hero!"

Dudwin waved and took off for the road.

Mordred crawled out from under the bush. He held up the gold coin. "Got it!" he cried.

"Excuse me, sir?" Erica said.

"What now?" Mordred asked as he got to his feet.

"We Bloodhounds found Seetha's gold," Erica said. "So we should get the prize."

"Oh! You want a prize, do you?" Mordred showed all his teeth in a fierce grin. "And so you shall have one!"

Wiglaf didn't like the way Mordred said that.

"Student teachers!" Mordred called. "Take the rest of the day off."

"Oh, thank you, sir!" cried the thin ones.

Mordred stomped over to his throne-like chair. He sat down.

"Wiglaf, for your prize, take the right front pole!" he ordered. "Eric, left front! Angus, you take the two in the rear! Pick me up all at once, boys. No bouncing!"

Wiglaf struggled to pick up his part of the large headmaster. He groaned as he took a step.

"Faster, boys!" Mordred cried. "Or we shall never make it home by nightfall!"

"Things could be worse," Erica said bravely as they staggered toward DSA.

Wiglaf nodded. And once they got there, he thought, they probably would be. But for now

Wiglaf felt glad that he had sent his brother home with a gold coin. And with a true story about Wiglaf, the hero.

This time he started the singing:

"We're the mighty Bloodhounds!
We're dogged and we're bold!
We're the mighty Bloodhounds!
And we found Seetha's gold!"

~DSA~
YEARBOOK

Goldius est goodius!

The Campus of Dragon Slayers' Academy

DSA

Lady Lobelia's Chamber

Dr. Pluck's Science Lab

Tunnel Exit

Mordred's Classroom

Headmaster's Office

Dining Hall

To Dungeon

Scrubbing Class

Stable

Castle Yard

Practice Dragon

Yorick's Quick Change-O-Rama

Camp Site

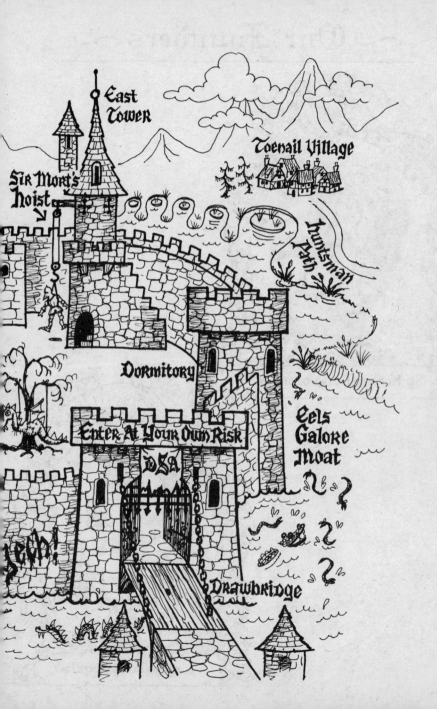

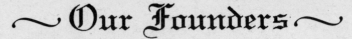

~Our Founders~

Sir Herbert Dungeonstone

Sir Ichabod Popquiz

~ Our Philosophy ~

Sir Herbert and Sir Ichabod founded Dragon Slayers' Academy on a simple principle still held dear today: Any lad—no matter how weak, yellow-bellied, lazy, pigeon-toed, smelly, or unwilling—can be transformed into a fearless dragon slayer who goes for the gold. After four years at DSA, lads will finally be of some worth to their parents, as well as a source of great wealth to this distinguished academy.* ** ***

* Please note that Dragon Slayers' Academy is a strictly-for-profit institution.

** Dragon Slayers' Academy reserves the right to keep some of the gold and treasure that any student recovers from a dragon's lair.

*** The exact amount of treasure given to a student's family is determined solely by our esteemed headmaster, Mordred. The amount shall be no less than 1/500th of the treasure and no greater than 1/499th.

~ Our Headmaster ~

Mordred de Marvelous

Mordred graduated from Dragon Bludgeon High, second in his class. The other student, Lionel Flyzwattar, went on to become headmaster of Dragon Stabbers' Prep. Mordred spent years as part-time, semi-substitute student teacher at Dragon Whackers' Alternative School, all the while pursuing his passion for mud wrestling. Inspired by how filthy rich Flyzwattar had become by running a school, Mordred founded Dragon Slayers' Academy in CMLXXIV, and has served as headmaster ever since.

❦

Known to the Boys as: Mordred de Miser
Dream: Piles and piles of dragon gold
Reality: Yet to see a single gold coin
Best-Kept Secret: Mud wrestled under the name Macho-Man Mordie
Plans for the Future: Will retire to the Bahamas . . . as soon as he gets his hands on a hoard

Lady Lobelia

Lobelia de Marvelous is Mordred's sister and a graduate of the exclusive If-You-Can-Read-This-You-Can-Design-Clothes Fashion School. Lobelia has offered fashion advice to the likes of King Felix the Husky and Eric the Terrible Dresser. In CMLXXIX, Lobelia married the oldest living knight, Sir Jeffrey Scabpicker III. That's when she gained the title of Lady Lobelia, but—alas!—only a very small fortune, which she wiped out in a single wild shopping spree. Lady Lobelia has graced Dragon Slayers' Academy with many visits, and can be heard around campus saying, "Just because I live in the Middle Ages doesn't mean I have to look middle-aged."

❧

Known to the Boys as: Lady Lo Lo
Dream: Frightfully fashionable
Reality: Frightful
Best-Kept Secret: Shops at Dark-Age Discount Dress Dungeon
Plans for the Future: New uniforms for the boys with mesh tights and lace tunics

~ Our Faculty ~

Sir Mort du Mort

Sir Mort is our well-loved professor of Dragon Slaying for Beginners as well as Intermediate and Advanced Dragon Slaying. Sir Mort says that, in his youth, he was known as the Scourge of Dragons. (We're not sure what it means, but it sounds scary.) His last encounter was with the most dangerous dragon of them all: Knight-shredder. Early in the battle, Sir Mort took a nasty blow to his helmet and has never been the same since.

Known to the Boys as: The Old Geezer
Dream: Outstanding Dragon Slayer
Reality: Just plain out of it
Best-Kept Secret: He can't remember
Plans for the Future: Taking a little nap

Coach Wendell Plungett

Coach Plungett spent many years questing in the Dark Forest before joining the Athletic Department at DSA. When at last he strode out of the forest, leaving his dragon-slaying days behind him, Coach Plungett was the most muscle-bulging, physically fit, manliest man to be found anywhere north of Nowhere Swamp. "I am what you call a hunk," the coach admits. At DSA, Plungett wears a number of hats—or, helmets. Besides PE Teacher, he is Slaying Coach, Square-Dance Director, Pep-Squad Sponsor, and Privy Inspector. He hopes to meet a damsel—she needn't be in distress—with whom he can share his love of heavy metal music and long dinners by candlelight.

Known to the Boys as: Coach
Dream: Tough as nails
Reality: Sleeps with a stuffed dragon named Foofoo
Best-Kept Secret: Just pull his hair
Plans for the Future: Finding his lost lady love

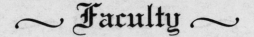

Brother Dave

Brother Dave is the DSA librarian. He belongs to the Little Brothers of the Peanut Brittle, an order known for doing impossibly good deeds and cooking up endless batches of sweet peanut candy. How exactly did Brother Dave wind up at Dragon Slayers' Academy? After a batch of his extra-crunchy peanut brittle left three children from Toenail toothless, Brother Dave vowed to do a truly impossible good deed. Thus did he offer to be librarian at a school world-famous for considering reading and writing a complete and utter waste of time. Brother Dave hopes to change all that.

❖

Known to the Boys as: Bro Dave
Dream: Boys reading in the libary
Reality: Boys sleeping in the library
Best-Kept Secret: Uses Cliff's Notes
Plans for the Future: Copying out all the lyrics to "Found a Peanut" for the boys

Professor Prissius Pluck

Professor Pluck graduated from Peter Piper Picked a Peck of Pickled Peppers Prep, and went on to become a professor of Science at Dragon Slayers' Academy. His specialty is the Multiple Choice Pop Test. The boys who take Dragon Science, Professor Pluck's popular class,

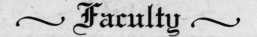

a) are amazed at the great quantities of saliva Professor P. can project
b) try never to sit in the front row
c) beg Headmaster Mordred to transfer them to another class
d) all of the above

⚜

Known to the Boys as: Old Spit Face
Dream: Proper pronunciation of *p*'s
Reality: Let us spray
Best-Kept Secret: Has never seen a pippi-hippo-pappa-peepus up close
Plans for the Future: Is working on a cure for chapped lips

Frypot

How Frypot came to be the cook at DSA is something of a mystery. Rumors abound. Some say that when Mordred bought the broken-down castle for his school, Frypot was already in the kitchen and he simply stayed on. Others say that Lady Lobelia hired Frypot because he was so speedy at washing dishes. Still others say Frypot knows many a dark secret that keeps him from losing his job. But no one ever, *ever* says that Frypot was hired because of his excellent cooking skills.

Known to the Boys as: Who needs a nickname with a real name like Frypot?

Dream: Cleaner kitchen

Reality: Kitchen cleaner

Best-Kept Secret: Takes long bubble baths in the moat

Plans for the Future: Has signed up for a beginning cooking class

Yorick

Yorick is Chief Scout at DSA. His knack for masquerading as almost anything comes from his years with the Merry Minstrels and Dancing Damsels Players, where he won an award for his role as the Glass Slipper in "Cinderella". However, when he was passed over for the part of Mama Bear in "Goldilocks", Yorick decided to seek a new way of life. He snuck off in the night and, by dawn, still dressed in the bear suit, found himself walking up Huntsmans Path. Mordred spied him from a castle window, recognized his talent for disguise, and hired him as Chief Scout on the spot.

Known to the Boys as: Who's that?
Dream: Master of Disguise
Reality: Mordred's Errand Boy
Best-Kept Secret: Likes dressing up as King Ken
Plans for the Future: To lose the bunny suit

Wiglaf of Pinwick

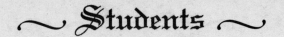

Wiglaf, our newest lad, hails from a hovel outside the village of Pinwick, which makes Toenail look like a thriving metropolis. Being one of thirteen children, Wiglaf had a taste of dorm life before coming to DSA and he fit right in. He started the year off with a bang when he took a stab at Coach Plungett's brown pageboy wig. Way to go, Wiggie! We hope to see more of this lad's wacky humor in the years to come.

❖

Dream: Bold Dragon-Slaying Hero
Reality: Still hangs on to a "security" rag
Extracurricular Activities: Animal-Lovers Club, President; No More Eel for Lunch Club, President; Frypot's Scrub Team, Brush Wielder; Pig Appreciation Club, Founder
Favorite Subject: Library
Oft-Heard Saying: *"Ello-hay, Aisy-day!"*
Plans for the Future: To go for the gold!

Angus du Pangus

The nephew of Mordred and Lady Lobelia, Angus walks the line between saying, "I'm just one of the lads" and "I'm going to tell my uncle!" Will this Class I lad ever become a mighty dragon slayer? Or will he take over the kitchen from Frypot some day? We of the DSA Yearbook staff are betting on choice #2. And hey, Angus? The sooner the better!

⚜

Dream: A wider menu selection at DSA
Reality: Eel, Eel, Eel!
Extracurricular Activities: DSA Cooking Club, President; Smilin' Hal's Off-Campus Eatery, Sales Representative
Favorite Subject: Lunch
Oft-Heard Saying: *"I'm still hungry"*
Plans for the Future: To write *101 Ways to Cook a Dragon*

Eric von Royale

Eric hails from Someplace Far Away (at least that's what he wrote on his Application Form). There's an air of mystery about this Class I lad, who says he is "totally typical and absolutely average." If that is so, how did he come to own the rich tapestry that hangs over his cot? And are his parents really close personal friends of Sir Lancelot? Did Frypot the cook bribe him to start the Clean Plate Club? And doesn't Eric's arm ever get tired from raising his hand in class so often?

❖

Dream: Valiant Dragon Slayer
Reality: Teacher's Pet
Extracurricular Activities: Sir Lancelot Fan Club; Armor Polishing Club; Future Dragon Slayer of the Month Club; DSA Pep Squad, Founder and Cheer Composer
Favorite Subject: All of Them!!!!!
Oft-Heard Saying: *"When I am a mighty Dragon Slayer . . ."*
Plans for the Future: To take over DSA

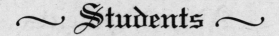

~ Students ~

Baldrick de Bold

This is a banner year for Baldrick. He is celebrating his tenth year as a Class I lad at DSA. Way to go, Baldrick! If any of you new students want to know the ropes, Baldrick is the one to see. He can tell when you should definitely *not* eat the cafeteria's eel, where the choice seats are in Professor Pluck's class, and what to tell the headmaster if you are late to class. Just don't ask him the answer to any test questions.

❦

Dream: To run the world
Reality: A runny nose
Extracurricular Activities: Practice Dragon Maintenance Squad; Least Improved Slayer-in-Training Award
Favorite Subject: *"Could you repeat the question?"*
Oft Heard Saying: *"A dragon ate my homework."*
Plans for the Future: To transfer to Dragon Stabbers' Prep

~ Advertisements ~